NINJA MEERKATS

For Matthew and Christopher Jones
~ G P J

STRIPES PUBLISHING
An imprint of Magi Publications
1 The Coda Centre, 189 Munster Road,
London SW6 6AW

A paperback original
First published in Great Britain in 2011

Text copyright © Gareth P. Jones, 2011
Illustrations copyright © Luke Finlayson, 2011
Cover illustration copyright © Domingos de Aquino, 2011

ISBN: 978-1-84715-192-6

A CIP catalogue record for this book is available
from the British Library.

Printed and bound in the UK.

6 8 10 9 7

NINJA MEERKATS

THE CLAN OF THE SCORPION

GARETH P. JONES

Stripes

There is an old meerkat proverb that goes:

Only the fattest pelican will wink at the unsuspecting turtle.

But, of course, we are neither pelicans nor are we turtles. We are meerkats. And what would meerkats want with being winked at? It is not something we care for. Like a blunt pencil, we simply can't see the point of it.

But I should not be wasting your time with a saying that has nothing to do with anything. Instead, I should be introducing you to...

The Clan of the Scorpion: four mighty warriors as strong and powerful as any ninja, all ready to risk their lives to save the world from our deadly enemy, the Ringmaster, a shadowy figure who runs an evil circus of goons and seeks to bring the world to its knees.

Jet Flashfeet: a super fast ninja whose only fault is craving the glory he so richly deserves.

Bruce "the muscle" Willowhammer: the strongest of the gang, though in the brain race he lags somewhat behind.

Donnie Dragonjab: a brilliant mind, inventor and master of gadgets.

Chuck Cobracrusher: his clear leadership has saved the others' skins more times than I care to remember.

Oh, and me, Grandmaster One-Eye: as old and wise as the sand dunes themselves.

There is not much else to tell you about this adventure except that I never did see my sink plunger again.

I will leave you with a poem by the ancient meerkat poet, Turner Frase.

> **When the wind blows west**
> **The wind blows best.**
> **When the wind blows south**
> **Sand gets in your mouth**
> **And in your ears**
> **And your belly button.**

Enough wisdom now. Sit back and enjoy the story of...

THE CLAN OF THE SCORPION.

CHAPTER ONE

THE MISSING TIGER

From the outside, the Clan of the Scorpion's secret base looked like one of a number of meerkat burrows in the Red Desert. But while some of the neighbouring meerkats had welcomed wildlife documentary makers into their homes, the Clan had to be more careful about who they let in.

You see, film crews do not expect to find a central chamber filled with fighting staffs, swords, throwing stars, nunchucks and a whole range of other gadgets at the heart of a meerkat burrow.

So the Clan kept nosy film-makers at arm's length for fear of their true identity being revealed... Actually, further than that, as a meerkat's arm is hardly very long at all.

Jet Flashfeet had just entered the central chamber. He had his trusty nunchucks in a specially designed holster, and was carrying a book under his arm called *101 More Martial Arts Moves* by Kara T. Kick. "Hey, who wants to try out this new move I just read about?"

"Not me. I'm busy with this," replied Donnie Dragonjab, tapping away on a touchpad phone he had recently acquired from a careless documentary maker.

Bruce Willowhammer looked up from the middle of the chamber, where he was doing one-armed push-ups. "What *is* that, Donnie?" he asked.

"It's a Bluetooth WAP-enabled mobile device," replied Donnie.

Bruce stopped mid push-up and stared at him blankly.

"It's a phone," explained Donnie.

"We've already got phones," said Bruce. With his free arm he pulled out the mini mobile phone that Donnie had made for each Clan member so that they could keep in contact during missions.

"You'll be able to throw away that old thing once I've figured out how to reduce this down to a more usable size," said Donnie. "This can surf the internet and give us up-to-date news from around the world with a simple click of a button. It's going to completely revolutionize the way we work."

Jet rolled his eyes impatiently. "Sounds great. Now, Bruce, will you try this new move with me?"

"All right, but can I have a snack first? I'm starving."

"You're always starving. Can't you wait? The helicopter leap will only take a minute," replied Jet.

"The what?" said Bruce.

"The helicopter leap. We link paws and spin round, then I count to three and we jump together and – Ninja-boom! – we fly up into the air like a helicopter."

"Why would we want to do that?"

"Because it's cool and it might come in handy."

"That's good enough for me. Let's do it," said Bruce.

"I have to see this." Donnie swivelled round to watch.

Jet and Bruce moved to the middle of the room. They stood on their hind legs, looked from side to side, then bowed to each other in the usual manner. They held paws, leaned back and began to move slowly round in a circle.

"Shall I put some music on?" said Donnie, sniggering at the sight of stocky, muscular Bruce apparently dancing with nimble, lean Jet.

Jet ignored him. "Faster now," he said. "And try not to tread on my feet."

"Sorry," Bruce mumbled.

They sped up, moving faster and faster until Jet yelled, "Jump!"

For a moment it looked like it was going to work. The two meerkats lifted off the ground, spinning in mid-air, but suddenly they whirled out of control, whizzing across the floor and knocking over a pile of weapons and tools in the process.

"Whooahhh!" cried Bruce.

"If that's what a helicopter is like, I think I'll stick to planes," said Donnie laughing, as Bruce and Jet came to a halt in a confused heap by the entrance to the chamber.

Just then, Chuck Cobracrusher, the fourth member and leader of the Clan, appeared.

"The helicopter leap requires much practice," he said, stepping over Jet and Bruce. "Few achieve it on their first try."

"It was his fault. He's too heavy," said Jet, springing to his feet. He pulled out a comb and straightened the fur on top of his head.

"No, Jet, that is not the problem. You are too hasty. Given time you will master this move," said Chuck. "Another new gadget, Donnie?"

"It's a blue-toothed whack-a-table phone," said Bruce, butting in.

"A Bluetooth, WAP-enabled phone," corrected Donnie. "It's amazing. I'm surfing the net right now."

"Technology is no substitute for the traditional ninja ways, but it can be useful," Chuck admitted. He brushed his fur back from his face, revealing the cross-shaped scar below his eye. He had never told the others how he had come by the scar; all they knew was that it had been inflicted by their deadly enemy, the Ringmaster, many years ago.

"Perhaps you can look up something for me, Donnie," said Chuck. "A tiger has gone missing from Hong Kong Zoo."

Donnie typed a few words into a search engine and found a news article.

"Here it is. It says that Ming, a rare speckle-white tigress, went missing last night from the zoo and that the police have no leads as to who may have taken her. How did you know about this, Chuck?"

"My brother, Throw, lives at the zoo and he has been keeping an eye on Ming for me. He called just now to give me the news."

"Your brother lives in a zoo?" said Bruce.

"Throw was never one for life in the wild. He prefers the conveniences of zoo life," replied Chuck. "He would have called earlier, but he had to wait until the zoo closed to use the payphone. Ming's disappearance is of great significance."

"A missing cat?" Jet shrugged. "Surely they'll just stick a sign on a tree like everyone else?"

Chuck shook his head. "Ming is no ordinary tiger. She once belonged to my old samurai master, Luhk Hu Stalking. She was trained by Master Stalking and is the only living tiger capable of..." he paused, then said dramatically, "...the Roar of Victory."

"Is that what you'd use to win a rowing boat race?" smirked Donnie.

"*Roar*, not oar," replied Chuck. "Whoever hears it is instantly put into a trance and must do the bidding of the next voice he or she hears. Master Stalking was wise and only ever used it in extreme cases and always for good. Since he died, Ming has lived safely in the zoo, her power kept a secret. But it seems that someone has discovered her past. And I can think of at least one person who would want to get his hands on her."

"The Ringmaster," said Jet.

Chuck nodded. "Our deadly enemy certainly has a fascination for things with great power."

"If he is behind this then we have no time to lose," said Jet.

"This time your haste is well placed," said Chuck. "I shudder to think of the damage he could do with such power. We must travel to Hong Kong at once. I will inform Grandmaster One-Eye of our departure."

The four meerkats bowed to one another, then leaped into action. Another death-defying mission was about to begin.

CHAPTER TWO

THE MEER-KART

Ten minutes later, four meerkat heads appeared above ground, each cautiously checking that the coast was clear. As the Clan slipped out of their burrow, a fifth head appeared.

"Ah, Chuck said you were off on an adventure," said Grandmaster One-Eye. "Would you like to know what the ancient philosopher, Paul the Other One, said about tigers?"

Donnie, Jet and Bruce sighed. They had heard much of the Grandmaster's so-called wisdom before, but Chuck, who had more respect for the old meerkat, asked, "What did he say, Grandmaster?"

"He asked the question, why do lions and tigers make such good shopkeepers? Because they always do a roaring trade." Grandmaster One-Eye snorted at his own joke. "Do not underestimate the power of laughter on a mission such as this."

"Wise words, Grandmaster." Chuck bowed and turned to the others. "Time to go," he said.

"I don't get it," said Bruce.

"I'll explain it on the way," said Jet. "So, how are we getting to Hong Kong, Chuck?"

"By plane. Which means we need to get to the airport. Donnie, have you repaired the Meer-kart?"

"Mostly," Donnie replied. He ducked behind a rock and pulled out what was little more than a large plank of wood and two sets of rickety wheels. Lying on top was a huge, scruffy brown suitcase, which made the kart sag in the middle.

"What's that?" asked Jet.

"That's my luggage," replied Donnie.

"Why do you always pack so much?" asked Bruce. "All I've brought are a few bags of deep fried lizard tails for the journey."

"This suitcase is for more important things than snacks," said Donnie. "Wait till you see my new disguise."

"Right," said Chuck, taking charge. "Bruce and Jet, you push first, and Donnie and I will steer."

"You always say that," moaned Bruce, "and we never get to swap."

Chuck ignored him and climbed on in front of Donnie.

Jet and Bruce stood on their hind legs and held on to the back of the kart.

"Let's go," shouted Chuck.

Jet and Bruce began to run, pushing the Meer-kart up a sand dune. At the top they jumped onboard and the kart hurtled down the other side, creating great clouds of sand behind them. They continued in this way through the desert, until finally the airport came into view.

"Go slow now. We want this thing to last," shouted Chuck.

"What did he say?" yelled Jet, who was struggling to hear over the sound of the rattling wheels.

"I think he said, 'Don't slow down. We want this thing to go fast,'" replied Bruce, as they powered the kart up the last dune.

"OK," said Jet. "Push!"

Bruce and Jet ran as fast as they could, then leaped aboard.

"I said *slow down*," yelled Chuck, as the Meer-kart hurtled towards the wire fence surrounding the airport. "Donnie, use the brakes."

"You know how I said I *mostly* repaired it?" shouted Donnie.

"Yes."

"Well, that was the bit I didn't fix."

"We've got no brakes?" cried Chuck. "Clan of the Scorpion, abandon Meer-kart!"

All four meerkats leaped off. Jet did a

spectacular somersault and a perfect landing. Bruce thudded to the ground with such force that he made a huge hole in the sand. Donnie used the suitcase to cushion his fall, and Chuck landed in an expert roll. They all shot up on to their hind legs and turned to watch as the kart crashed into the fence, splintering into pieces.

"Don't worry," said Donnie. "I'll fix it when we get back."

"Yes and perhaps next time, Donnie, remember to fix the brakes," replied Chuck.

If you have ever boarded a plane you may have noticed a distinct lack of meerkats running around the airport. And the Clan's nearest airport was no exception, because instead of four meerkats slipping through the automatic door, a scruffy brown suitcase entered. It moved closely behind a smart-looking businessman, leading all to assume he was pulling it along with his other bag. No one noticed the four pairs of feet that scuttled along underneath, nor the tiny eyeholes in the side of the case.

Chuck looked up at the Departures board. "There's a flight to Hong Kong leaving in three hours. Check-in is right here."

The suitcase peeled away from the businessman and joined the check-in queue for the Hong Kong flight. Slowly, it shuffled along with the other cases, unnoticed by the old lady in front.

"So far so good," said Chuck. "Now we need to distract this passenger so that we can check in as one of her bags. Any ideas?"

"Leave it to me," said Jet, slipping out from under the suitcase.

"Jet, wait!" cried Chuck.

But Jet had already scuttled up the side of the suitcases in front, to where he could see the old lady's passport sticking out of her coat pocket. He picked it up in his teeth, darted round and dropped it into her other pocket, then returned to the case.

"See, no problem," said Jet.

"You could have been seen," said Chuck. "You must learn to think before you act."

The man at the desk looked up. "Next."

The old lady reached to get her passport and was surprised to find her pocket empty.

"That's odd. I'm sure I put it in there." As she checked her other pockets, the scruffy brown suitcase jumped on to the scales beside the desk. "Ah, here it is," she said. She gave it to the man and placed her luggage on the scales.

"Is this everything?" asked the man.

"Yes, that's all."

The man labelled the bags and handed the lady her boarding pass. As the luggage moved off on the conveyer belt, she had no idea that she had just checked in a suitcase full of meerkats.

The Clan was on its way.

CHUCKY EGG

It was a hot, sticky evening in Hong Kong and, as the plane landed, the sun was just disappearing behind the skyscrapers that filled the city. On one side of the plane the passengers walked down a flight of stairs. On the other, the baggage handlers unloaded the suitcases on to a trolley. No one noticed one of the cases rattle itself off the trolley and make its way to the side of the runway.

"What now?" asked Bruce.

"My brother is meeting us on the east side of the car park," said Chuck.

"Let's go then," said Jet, slipping out from under the case.

"Get back inside," ordered Chuck. "We must remain under cover. If any one of us is seen we could endanger the entire mission."

"But it's so hot in here," Jet grumbled, sliding back underneath. "And it stinks of fried lizard tails, thanks to Bruce."

"As my mum always says, there's no such thing as a bad food smell," said Bruce.

"Having smelled your mum's cricket stew, I'd have to disagree," replied Donnie.

They made their way to the car park, and peered through the eyeholes.

"Where is he then?" asked Jet.

"Perhaps he has lost his way," said Chuck. "It's getting dark and this is his first time out of the zoo. Jet and Bruce, you stay hidden here in case he turns up. Donnie and I will take the suitcase and go and look for him.

And remember, if our hunch is right and
the Ringmaster has something to do with
Ming's disappearance, he and his henchmen
may well be expecting us ... and they won't
be throwing us a welcome party..."

"So we just sit about and do nothing?"
grumbled Jet.

"Jet, like a pop singer considering a new
career, you need to learn that sometimes it
is better not to act," said
Chuck. "No more
impetuous behaviour."

Chuck and Donnie
headed off inside the
case.

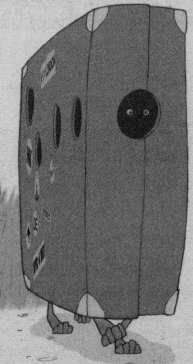

"What does 'impetuous' mean?" asked Bruce.

"It means I'm ready to spring into action," said Jet. "Which is what I'm going to do now. Come on, let's go and look for Throw so we can get on with our mission."

"But Chuck said we had to stay here," said Bruce. "And he *is* the leader."

"What are you, a mouse or a meerkat?" said Jet, scurrying off through the grass. "It won't do any harm. It's not like we'll get *seen*. Come on!"

Donnie and Chuck directed the suitcase through the car park, darting behind cars every time a human appeared.

"Jet is a talented ninja but he is too much like a trainee doctor," said Chuck, as they took cover behind a car.

"In what way?" asked Donnie.

"He has much to learn about patience," replied Chuck, with a wry smile.

"Argh!" came a voice beside them. "Talking luggage? Now I really have seen it all. The sooner I'm back in the zoo, the better."

"Throw!" said Chuck, seeing his brother's head poking out from beside one of the car's wheels.

"What?" yelped Throw, quivering with fright. "Talking luggage that knows my name! Help!"

Chuck leaped out from under the suitcase. "It's me, Chuck, your brother."

Throw gaped at him. "Chucky Egg! Am I glad to see you," he cried, clasping his arms round his brother.

Donnie sniggered. "Chucky Egg?"

Chuck scowled at his brother, his face

reddening under his fur. "Throw, please.
I am the leader of an elite ninja clan. I do
not go by that name any more."

"Sorry, Chucky ... I mean Chuck,"
said Throw. "But I'm so glad to see you.
I thought I'd never find you. The outside
world is terrifying ... and confusing. You
said it was a park, but there are no trees."

"It's a *car* park," said Chuck. "For cars. Never mind, we've found you now. Did you manage to arrange transport for us?"

"Yes, a van from the zoo is here to collect a pair of sloths. It's leaving shortly," Throw replied. "It'll be easy to slip aboard."

"Good work," said Chuck. "Let's go and pick up the others."

The journey back to the eastern corner of the car park took twice as long with Throw's help, as he kept trying to push the suitcase in the wrong direction. When they arrived, Jet and Bruce were nowhere to be seen.

"No doubt Jet has convinced Bruce to do something impetuous," said Chuck. "Jet is a great fighter but he is also like a car with no steering wheel."

"In what way?" asked Throw.

"Almost impossible to control," replied Chuck. "Come on. They can't have gone far."

CHAPTER FOUR

IMPETUOUS JET

On the other side of the car park, Jet had spotted something interesting.

"Bruce, look at that car," he said.

"Oh yeah, it's right across two spaces. That's bad parking," said Bruce.

"Not the parking," said Jet. "The car itself."

Jet was pointing at an orange car with multicoloured spots, bright purple hubcaps and a ridiculously large exhaust pipe.

"It's the clowns' car," said Bruce.

"Exactly," said Jet. "Looks like Grimsby

and Sheffield, the Ringmaster's henchmen, are in town. And there's Grimsby now."

The car door opened and a large yellow shoe appeared, followed by a clown wearing a red costume. He had a sad painted face and green hair sprouting from under his hat. Another clown climbed out of the other side. He was wearing a blue wig and his mouth had been painted with a big smile. They both wore fake red noses. They hurried off as fast as their huge feet would allow.

"Looks like Chuck was right," said Jet. "The circus is in town at the exact same time a powerful tigress goes missing. What a coincidence! Let's take a closer look."

"Shouldn't we find the others first?" asked Bruce.

Jet shook his head. "We need to find out what they're up to. Besides, I expect Chuck and Donnie are still looking for Chuck's brother. You know what zoo animals are like. Without a YOU ARE HERE sign they don't know where they are."

"I suppose it won't hurt to have a quick look," said Bruce. He followed Jet to the car.

"Ah good. It's locked," said Jet.

"What do you mean good?" asked Bruce.

"I've been looking for a chance to practise my Air-Key Open Palm Move," said Jet. "And this is perfect."

"Your *what*?"

"I read about it in *What Karate!* last week. It involves a non-impact punch that twists the air itself into the lock and opens the door."

Jet took a step back and raised his flattened palm. Then he leaped forward and launched himself at the boot, stopping right in front of it and twisting his paw.

It looked impressive, but when he tried the boot it was still locked.

"I must have twisted the air the wrong way," said Jet.

"My go," announced Bruce. "Time for some Bruce Force."

Using the exhaust pipe as a springboard, Bruce jumped up and whacked the boot.

It sprang open with a twang.

"Very effective," Jet admitted. "Though totally lacking in style. Now, let's look for clues."

"Like what?" asked Bruce.

"Something that links those clowns to the theft of the tiger," said Jet.

Bruce climbed into the boot and glanced around. "There's nothing except for this cage, this empty box of meat and half a packet of sleeping pills."

Jet sprang up and joined him. "This is too easy," he chuckled. "They must've crushed up the sleeping pills with the meat to knock Ming out, then transported her in the cage."

"Oh yeah, I didn't think of that," said Bruce. "But this cage is way too small for a tiger, isn't it?"

"Eh up, looks like we have a little pest problem," said a voice behind them.

"And they've walked right into our trap just like the Ringmaster said they would. Good thing we bought a job lot of these cages."

The meerkats spun round to see Grimsby step out from the shadows. "Shame there's only two of them, though."

"Never mind, we'll get the other two later," said Sheffield, appearing next to him.

"No one cages a meerkat. Ninja-boom!" cried Jet, leaping up and kicking Sheffield straight in the nose, which made a loud honking noise.

HONK!

Bruce followed Jet's lead with a punch to the clown's chest, ripping the pocket from his shirt. A massive spotty handkerchief fluttered out. Sheffield staggered back, but Grimsby was there in his place.

"Would you like to smell my flower?" he grinned, shoving the bright green flower on his lapel in the meerkats' faces. It was the kind that normally squirts water, but not today – a blue gas with a strong smell of rotten eggs sprayed out of the centre, enveloping the meerkats.

"That's lovely. What's it called?" asked Sheffield.

"Its Latin name is Knockouticus Gasicus," said Grimsby.

"Shame we can't smell a thing thanks to these protective noses," said Sheffield.

"Knock-out gas," uttered Jet, then he and Bruce fell unconscious.

Half an hour later, Jet and Bruce awoke to find themselves locked inside the cage in the boot of the clowns' car.

Bruce rubbed his head. "I told you we should have stayed put. Chuck's gonna go mad."

"All right, keep your fur on," said Jet. "I'll take the blame. Let's just concentrate on trying to find a way out of here."

He checked the bars of the cage, but they were too close together for them to slip through.

Bruce pulled out his phone. "We should call for help."

Suddenly, the car braked sharply, sending the cage sliding forward.

"Hold on," said Jet. "I can hear what they're saying."

"...The light show on New Year's Eve!" Grimsby chuckled.

"And that's when he'll use it?" replied Sheffield.

"Yes. That's why we're going to The Peak after we've disposed of these two."

"Sounds like it'll be a *roaring* success," said Sheffield. The two clowns laughed.

The van set off again, sending the cage flying into the boot door. Bruce lost his grip on his phone and it flew through the bars.

"Don't worry. I've still got mine," said Jet, reaching into his holster.

But before he could grab it, the car swung round a corner, screeched to a halt and Grimsby opened the boot.

"Eh up, little ninjas," said Sheffield, appearing next to him. "Welcome to Hong Kong docks. The perfect place to dispose of some pesky rodents without anyone seeing."

"I'm going to wipe that fake smile right off your face," Jet cried. "Ninja-boom!" He flicked out his claws and attempted to slice through the bars. Unfortunately, the bars didn't break.

"Maybe with some Bruce Force," said Bruce. He charged at the side and managed to bend the bars slightly.

The clowns laughed. "This cage is made out of titanium," said Sheffield. "A material strong enough to hold far bigger creatures than you, my furry little friends."

"What does the Ringmaster plan to do on New Year's Eve?" demanded Jet.

"Yeah, is he going to have a party? That's what most people do," said Bruce.

"That's not what I meant," said Jet.

"You should be more concerned with what we're planning to do to *you*!" Grimsby grinned. "Prepare to swim with the fishes."

"Except you won't be swimming," added Sheffield.

"No," Grimsby agreed. "More like drowning." He picked up the cage and dangled it over the murky water.

"Hey, Grimsby, how does the sea say goodbye?" asked Sheffield.

"I don't know, Sheffield, how *does* the sea say goodbye?"

"It doesn't. It just waves."

Grimsby hooted with laughter and dropped the cage. It hit the water with a huge splash and sunk out of sight.

CHAPTER FIVE

A CLUE AT THE ZOO
(IN THE POO)

Hong Kong has one of the deepest harbours in the world, so Bruce had plenty of time to reflect on his life as he and Jet sank to their almost certain death. Mostly, he found himself regretting not having eaten more. Sure, he had eaten quite a bit, but if he had cut out sleeping and really focused on it, he reckoned he could probably have eaten at least twice as much.

Jet, on the other hand, wasn't going down without a fight. He held on to the cage with his paw to steady himself, and positioned his other paw in front of the lock with his palm facing forward. Bruce floated over to see what he was doing. He watched as Jet raised his palm and thrust himself towards the lock. To Bruce's surprise, the cage door swung open. Jet burst through, quickly followed by Bruce.

They broke the surface, coughing and spluttering, and swam to the bank.

"How did you open the cage?" asked Bruce, gasping for breath.

"I remembered that the Air-Key Open Palm Move works better when used under water," replied Jet. "And this time I twisted the right way."

Back in the airport, Donnie, Chuck and Throw had found no trace of Jet and Bruce. "They're not answering their phones either," said Donnie. "Something's up."

"You may be right," said Chuck. "But we must continue with the mission and wait for them to contact us. Jet may get himself into trouble a lot, but he is very capable of getting himself out of it again. Throw, take us to this zoo van you spoke of."

The battered suitcase set off across the car park once more and was soon safely tucked inside the van. The meerkats wriggled out from underneath their disguise, and found themselves in the company of two sleepy sloths. As the van set off, Donnie emptied out the suitcase and repacked his stuff into a neat backpack. One of the sloths half opened one of its eyes for a second, glanced at him, then went back to sleep, which, if you know anything about sloths, is about as exciting as they get.

When they arrived at the zoo, Throw led Donnie and Chuck to Ming's cage. The zoo was quiet at night and they were able to move around without needing a disguise.

They slipped through the bars of the cage, and Chuck and Donnie set about checking it for clues.

"What are you looking for?" asked Throw.

"The police already searched it."

"Then no doubt they are now looking for a man with extremely large feet," said Chuck. "Look at this!"

In the middle of a pile of tiger dung was an enormous footprint.

"Surely only a giant would make such a big track," said Throw nervously.

"Not a giant," replied Donnie. "A clown."

"And I bet I know whose clown," said Chuck. "The Ringmaster's."

Suddenly, there was the sound of dramatic music.

"What's that?" asked Throw, jumping in fright.

Donnie pulled out his phone. "That's my new ringtone. Hello? Oh, hi, Jet."

"Where is he?" demanded Chuck.

"Hold on, I'll put it on speakerphone," replied Donnie.

"Jet, Bruce, why didn't you two answer your phones?" asked Chuck.

"Bruce lost his and mine stopped working after we were thrown into the harbour by Sheffield and Grimsby," replied Jet. "We're calling from a payphone. We caught a ferry into the city centre."

"So the clowns are in town," said Chuck. "Have you found out anything else?"

"Yeah," said Bruce. "Jet's Air-Key Open Palm Move works underwater."

"I'm glad to hear that," said Chuck. "But have you discovered anything of importance to our mission?"

"We overheard the clowns talking about a light show and New Year's Eve," said Jet.

Chuck turned to his brother. "Any idea what that means, Throw?"

"No idea," he replied.

Another voice came over the phone.

"Testing, one two, one two..."

"Who is that?" asked Chuck.

"I don't know. It's coming through a big speaker just above us," said Jet.

"Testing, one two..." said the voice. "This is the Hong Kong New Year's Celebration Commentary, broadcasting across the whole of the city for tonight's Chinese New Year light show, when the skyscrapers will light up the city and fireworks will light up the sky. For the best view in town, why not take the tram up to The Peak, 552 metres above sea level."

"The clowns also mentioned something about a peak," said Jet. "I think it's where the circus has set up camp."

"Then that's where we will go," said Chuck. "Meet us at the tram terminal. The nearest bin should provide adequate cover."

"OK," said Jet, ringing off.

"Throw, we must take our leave," said Chuck.

"But I want to come with you, Chucky Eg— I mean, Chuck," protested Throw.

Chuck shook his head. "As brothers, we were both born wild but your time in the zoo has tamed you. You are hand fed and the only danger you face is the possibility of a child mistaking you for a soft toy and cuddling you to death. For me, danger is as real as the scar on my face."

"Can't I help at all?" asked Throw.

"You already have. You alerted us to Ming's disappearance. Now, return to your cage knowing that you have played an important part in this mission."

The brothers hugged, then Chuck and Donnie took their leave.

CHAPTER SIX

JOURNEY TO THE PEAK

There was a long queue of people outside the tram terminal. Bruce and Jet were the first to arrive at the bin across the road, having stowed aboard a ferry from the dock, then used a newspaper as cover to make their way to the terminal. Donnie and Chuck had each donned a crisp packet on their heads by way of a disguise, but had been temporarily delayed by an overly eager litter collector, who had shovelled them into his bin.

"What are you eating?" Donnie asked Bruce when they arrived.

"Some kind of noodles, I think," Bruce replied, holding up the carton.

"You're eating food from bins?" said Donnie.

Bruce shrugged. "At least I'm not afraid of trying foreign foods."

"Well, I hope you like foreign illnesses, too."

"What now?" asked Jet, eager to get on.

"We go in disguise to The Peak," said Chuck. "Then we split up and search for the Ringmaster. Whatever he plans, we know he intends to do it tonight on New Year's Eve."

"Hang on, New Year's Eve was last month," said Bruce. "Remember, we all ate too many crickets and sang that song about the old lamb sign?" said Bruce.

"*Auld Lang Syne*," corrected Donnie.

"This is *Chinese* New Year," said Chuck.

"And this year they are celebrating the Year of the Tiger. Donnie, we need to get on that tram without being seen. The Ringmaster and his minions will be looking out for us. Any ideas?"

Donnie smiled. "I have just the thing." He pulled out something large and furry from his backpack.

"What is that?" asked Bruce.

"It's a brilliant disguise," said Donnie. "It has hollow legs and four sets of eyeholes in the body. I call it..." he paused for dramatic effect. "Puppy."

"Puppy?" said Jet.

"P.U.P.P.Y.," said Donnie. "Prototype Undercover Pretend Poodle Yoodle. Prototype because it's the first one. Undercover because that's what it's for. And Pretend Poodle explains itself."

"What about the Yoodle?"

"That's just to make it spell 'puppy'," replied Donnie.

"Won't a stuffed toy dog look more suspicious than just us as we are?" asked Jet.

Chuck shook his head. "The Ringmaster won't be looking out for a poodle," he replied. "Even a pretend one."

Jet looked unconvinced, but he knew he was outnumbered. He sighed and climbed into place as one of the puppy's legs.

The meerkats had to jump in time to make the puppy look like it was walking, but anyone watching closely would have noticed that one of the poodle's back legs was always out of time with the rest.

"Bruce, please keep up," said Donnie.

"Sorry, I was just finishing this spring roll."

"From the bin?"

"Where else?"

"Disgusting."

The odd-looking poodle moved through the crowds to the front of the tram queue. It quickly got rid of an over-friendly terrier with a swift whack from Jet's nunchucks, but an annoying little English boy on board was harder to scare off.

"Doggy," said the boy. "Look at the doggy, Mummy."

His mother ignored him.

"Doggy," he said, pulling its tail.

"Get out of it," snarled Bruce.

The child stared blankly at the dog.

"Talking doggy," he said.

"That's nice, dear," said his mother. "Now come along."

At The Peak, the meerkat-poodle followed everyone off the tram and headed for a spot with a good view of the brightly lit skyscrapers that towered over the city.

"Tonight, people all over the world will be watching this spectacular event," said the voice through the loudspeaker. "And on the ground there are performances and celebrations for everyone to enjoy."

The Peak was full of stalls selling strong-smelling food and glowing lanterns. In amongst them, street acts entertained the crowds.

"Hey, look, an acrobatic show. I love acrobats," said Bruce, suddenly stopping.

With one of its back legs rooted to the spot, the meerkat-poodle was brought to a standstill.

"Bruce, we don't have time for this," said Jet.

"Just a couple of minutes," said Bruce.
"It looks great."

Three Chinese men were performing
amazing acrobatics. They jumped on to
each other's shoulders, lifted each
other in the air, and performed triple
somersaults effortlessly, causing the
crowd to *Ooh* and *Ahh*. The smallest of
the men then scrambled up a long
pole with the speed and agility of
a monkey.

"Come on, Bruce,"
said Donnie. "We're
wasting time."

"Yes, Bruce, there is a time and a place for watching street performances," said Chuck. "And this is not it."

"But it's the big finish," said Bruce.

The largest of the three men stood with his arms outstretched, holding the other two, before they both flipped into the air, turned a somersault and landed by his side.

"Thank you," he said. "My name is Stan Ding and this is Wob Ling and Jum Ping." The other two acrobats bowed. "Please give generously if you enjoyed the show."

"Great, can we go now?" said Jet impatiently.

"Hold on, I want to get their autographs," said Bruce.

Suddenly, the meerkat-poodle found itself being dragged along by its back leg.

"Bruce, stop," said Donnie. "This isn't going to work. One, people don't just barge in asking for autographs. Two, we're on a secret mission to save the world and don't have time for this. And three, you're a meerkat disguised as the back leg of a poodle; they won't give you an autograph!"

"What was one again?" asked Bruce.

"Actually, I think Bruce's determination has paid off," said Chuck. "Look."

Through the eyeholes in the disguise, the others watched the three acrobats huddle together in conversation with a tall man wearing a big hat and an evil smile.

"The Ringmaster," said Donnie. "Bruce, I take it back. You're a genius."

"Thanks, Donnie," replied Bruce. "Now can I get their autographs?"

CHAPTER SEVEN

THE HELICOPTER LEAP

"We must approach with caution," said Chuck. "And listen in."

The meerkat-poodle inched forward, taking care to avoid the Ringmaster's loyal pet, Doris the Dancing Dog, who was sniffing a nearby lamp post.

"...Then you redirect it to my microphone," the Ringmaster was saying, as they drew closer. "Do you think you can do that, my flexible friends?"

"For what you're paying, it will be no problem," said Stan Ding.

The others nodded.

"What if these rodents you warned us about turn up?" asked one of the acrobats.

"Two have already been disposed of, thanks to my clowns," replied the Ringmaster. "You have permission to deal with the remaining pair as you see fit."

"Rodents?" said Bruce.

"Disposed of?" Jet grinned.

"Quiet," warned Chuck.

Doris looked up and eyed the poodle. Her nose twitched. She trotted over to it and stared into the poodle's eyes. The four meerkats froze on the spot.

"Woof," barked Doris.

"Woof," responded Donnie.

Doris gave the poodle a suspicious sniff.

"Come on, Doris, this is no time for making friends," said the Ringmaster. "Good luck, gentlemen. And remember, it must be done before the stroke of midnight, when everyone will be listening."

Doris threw the poodle one last glance and trotted over to her master. The Ringmaster turned and headed down the hill, with Doris by his side.

"That was close," whispered Jet. "I thought that mutt was going to ruin our cover."

"Donnie's disguise worked well," said Chuck. "Now, we must turn our attention to the matter in hand." He looked up at a nearby wooden pole. A wire ran across the top and into a nearby building. "I think I understand the Ringmaster's plan now," he said. "That wire must be for the speaker system we keep hearing. Those acrobats plan to climb this pole and redirect the system so the Ringmaster can take control of it. With that kind of amplification he could use the Roar of Victory to turn the whole city into his slaves in a second."

"Clever," said Jet.

"Donnie and Bruce, it's up to you to stop the acrobats. Jet, you come with me. We'll follow the Ringmaster."

Behind a nearby bush, the four meerkats climbed out of the dog disguise and bowed to one another.

"Good luck. Stay true to the Way of the Scorpion," said Chuck. "Come on, Jet."

As Chuck and Jet set off after the Ringmaster, Donnie and Bruce turned their attention to the three acrobats.

"So how are we going to do this?" asked Donnie. "We need a cunning, well-thought-out plan to overcome these flexible fiends and prevent them from climbing the pole and redirecting the communication line."

"What about this?" said Bruce. "Oi, acrobats, get ready for the fight of your lives!"

"Great," said Donnie, slapping his head in disbelief. "Not *quite* what I had in mind."

The acrobats turned round, but it took a while for them to notice who was speaking.

"Well, well, well. It's the rodents," said Stan Ding, glancing down.

"We're not rodents," said Bruce.

"That's right," said Donnie. "We're a kind of mongoose."

Donnie did a double spin and kicked Stan Ding in the shin with enough force to knock over an oak tree but which hardly bothered the muscly acrobat at all. Jum Ping and Wob Ling jumped up on to Stan Ding's shoulders and launched themselves at the meerkats.

"Bruce Force!" cried Bruce, kicking Jum Ping in the stomach.

Wob Ling tried to land a punch on Donnie but the meerkat dodged the attack, dived between his legs and hit him in the back.

"Ladies and gentlemen, three minutes until midnight," said the voice from the loudspeaker, as the battle raged.

As Bruce and Donnie fought the acrobats, Chuck and Jet followed the Ringmaster down the hill and into a shady park, where they found a high barbed-wire fence.

"How did they get through?" asked Jet.

"I don't know, but this fence has been designed to keep us out. The Ringmaster will have planted it deep in the soil, making it impossible to burrow under."

"What now?"

"We will perform the helicopter leap," said Chuck.

Jet gaped at him. "You saw what happened when I tried that before. We'll end up getting skewered!"

"Have faith, Jet. I will show you the correct way to execute the move. Now take my paws."

The two meerkats bowed to each other,
then crossed their arms, held paws and
began moving in a circle.

"Gradually increase your speed," said
Chuck. "Keep your feet evenly spaced.
Breathe deeply. Focus on my eyes."

They moved faster and faster until the black, red and yellow of their ninja clothes blurred into orange.

"On my count," shouted Chuck. "One... Two... Three!"

They leaped in the air and, like a helicopter, glided high up and over the fence, landing safely on the other side.

"That is how we perform the helicopter leap," said Chuck.

"Ninja-boom!" exclaimed Jet. "Now let's go and find the Ringmaster."

"There's no need," said a voice from the darkness. "The Ringmaster has already found you."

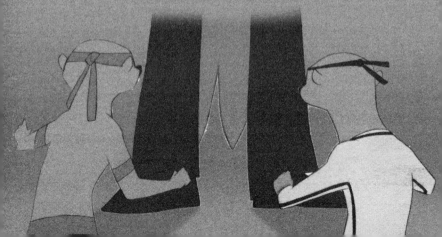

Jet and Chuck sprang into attack positions. Chuck drew his sword and Jet grabbed his nunchucks from his holster.

"Ladies and gentlemen, boys and girls," cried the Ringmaster, "for your fighting pleasure I'd like to introduce Jet Flashfeet and Chuck Cobracrusher, and their opponents... First up, they'll have you splitting your sides and literally dying with laughter, the clowns, Sheffield and Grimsby!" The two clowns stepped out of the shadows.

"Thought we'd seen the last of you at the dock," said Sheffield to Jet. "Not to worry, we'll do it properly this time."

"Next, Doris the Dancing Dog," continued the Ringmaster. "Doris is trained in the ways of the tango, the foxtrot, the quickstep and lethal combat."

"Is this all you've got? Two men in make-up and a mangy mutt with some weedy dance moves?" sneered Jet.

Doris snarled.

"You want more?" replied the Ringmaster.
"No problem! From the mountains of
Austria, may I present seven siblings who
will astonish you with their mid-air
manoeuvres... It's the Family Von Trapeze."

"*Ein, zwei, drei*, attack!" shouted a voice.

From the trees, seven trapeze artists
swung down towards Jet and Chuck.
Sheffield pulled out a frying pan and took a
swipe at Chuck. Grimsby did the same with
an oversized hammer. Meanwhile, Doris
turned an elegant pirouette into a powerful
spin kick.

"Let's go!" shouted Jet. He dodged Doris
and sprang into the air, somersaulting over
the clowns' heads. Next, he ran between
their legs and, with lightning speed, tied
their shoe laces together, causing them to
crash to the ground.

"Ninja-boom!" he cried.

Doris waltzed towards Chuck, barking
madly, as three members of the Von
Trapeze family swung at him from above.

Chuck ducked, kicked Doris in the jaw, and then used his sword to vault out of the way. The trapeze artists crashed into each other and tumbled to the floor but there were more where they came from. And now the clowns were back on their feet.

"Time to *wrap up* this situation," said the Ringmaster.

He cracked his whip, wrapping it tightly round Chuck, and pinning his sword to his side.

"Jet," said Chuck. "Like a snake trying to play tennis, I could do with a hand here."

"On my way," called Jet, swinging his nunchucks above his head to keep the clowns at bay. Suddenly, something nipped his back leg. He reached down to bat it away, and was immediately pulled to the ground by Doris.

"Oh dear. I'd say you two are well and

truly floored." The Ringmaster handed his whip to Sheffield and pulled a microphone from his inside pocket. "These celebrations are being broadcast across the world. In ten seconds, millions of people around the globe will be under my power. And there's nothing you vermin can do about it. Ah listen, the countdown has commenced."

"TEN..." said the voice through the loudspeaker. "NINE..."

"Grimsby, the lead, please."

Grimsby dived into the bushes and emerged holding a lead. He tugged it sharply and out of the darkness walked a speckle-white tigress.

CHAPTER EIGHT

THE YEAR OF THE TIGER

"EIGHT…" said the voice through the loudspeaker.

Back at The Peak, Donnie and Bruce were busy fighting Jum Ping and Stan Ding, as Wob Ling climbed up the pole towards the wire.

"SEVEN…"

"Bruce, it's time Jum Ping went flying and got Wob Ling toppling," said Donnie.

"You betcha," cried Bruce.

He darted under Stan Ding's legs and grabbed Jum Ping's right hand.

Donnie took hold of his left. The two meerkats jumped up on to Stan Ding's shoulders and flipped Jum Ping up over his head, propelling him into Wob Ling, and knocking him off the pole.

"SIX."

Stan Ding laughed. "It's too late. He's already redirected the line."

"FIVE."

Donnie cocked his ear. The voice doing the countdown had changed. It was now the menacingly mirthful mutterings of the Ringmaster. Quickly, Donnie pulled out a device from his backpack, made from a spring, some string, a washing-up bottle and a sink plunger, and took aim.

"FOUR."

"Hey, that's Grandmaster's sink plunger! He's been looking for that," said Bruce.

"THREE."

"No, you don't," said Stan Ding,
blocking his view.

"You're standing in the way," said Bruce.
He jumped up and landed on Stan Ding's
toes with all his might. The acrobat cried
out and crashed to the ground with a loud
THUD, clearing the way for Donnie to fire.

The plunger flew up into the air, and
looped over the wire.

"Bruce, pull!" shouted Donnie.

"TWO."

Bruce grabbed the plunger and pulled, snapping the wire that ran along the top.

"ONE!"

"Happy New Year," said Donnie. "Now, let's tie up the loose ends."

"My pleasure," said Bruce. He yanked the wire free and whizzed around, binding the three disorientated acrobats to the pole.

"Good work," said Donnie. "Let's go and find the others."

"Happy New Year, everyone. It's the Year of the Tiger, I'm the Ringmaster and this..." he grinned with evil delight, "...is the Roar of Victory!"

Beside the Ringmaster, the Family Von Trapeze quickly pushed earplugs into their ears. The clowns had used their hair and Sheffield had covered Doris's ears with his hands. But there was nothing to prevent Jet and Chuck from hearing the mighty roar that came from Ming's throat when the Ringmaster cracked his whip across her back.

Jet and Chuck instantly stopped struggling.

Their eyes glazed over.

"Aha!" cried the Ringmaster. "Victory is—Hold on..." He tapped the microphone angrily. "I can't hear myself through the speakers any more. Something's gone wrong. Who is responsible for this?"

No one said a word.

"Why is no one answering me?"

Still no one spoke.

"Unblock your ears, you fools," he snapped.

"Eh?" said Sheffield.

"What was zat?" asked the eldest of the Family Von Trapeze.

"I said, UNBLOCK YOUR EARS!" yelled the Ringmaster, reaching over and yanking the hair out of Grimsby's ears.

"There's no need to shout," said Grimsby.

"No doubt the other two meddling meerkats have disconnected the line," said the Ringmaster, purple with rage.

"Well, these two can fix it up again. Ninja meerkats, who do you obey?"

"We obey you," they replied as one.

The Ringmaster laughed. "Music to my ears! Release them."

The eldest Von Trapeze boy unwound the whip from around Chuck and handed it back to the Ringmaster, while Doris stepped off Jet.

Jet and Chuck stared on, unblinking.

"Not so fast, Ringmaster," said Donnie, appearing from behind a tree with Bruce by his side.

"Ah good, you've saved me the trouble of coming to find you. Our latest recruits will deal with you. Chuck Cobracrusher and Jet Flashfeet, destroy these meerkats."

"As you wish," replied Jet, raising his nunchucks.

"What are you doing, Jet?" said Bruce.

"They must have heard the Roar of Victory," said Donnie. "They're under the Ringmaster's spell."

"What? You mean we've got to fight our friends?" said Bruce.

"Looks that way," said Donnie.

With glazed eyes, Jet swung his nunchucks at Bruce, catching him off-guard and knocking him over.

The Ringmaster boomed with laughter at the sight of his sworn foes fighting each other. "Chuck, why are you not attacking?" he demanded.

Chuck turned to face him. "I am attacking." He jumped up and swung his sword, slicing cleanly through the leash that held Ming. Free at last, the tiger turned and ran into the surrounding trees. The Ringmaster tried to catch her with his whip, but Chuck cut through that too.

"What? How is this possible?"

"Ming belonged to my old master, Luhk Hu Stalking," said Chuck. "I spent many hours training and meditating in order to learn how to become immune to her roar."

"Ha, well I still have your best fighter. Jet, you can take them all on."

"Yes, master," replied Jet, preparing to strike.

"Best fighter?" said Bruce, dodging

another lunge from him. "Chuck, do I have permission to hit Jet now?"

"Hitting is not necessary," said Chuck. "As Grandmaster One-Eye has told us, we have more powerful weapons at our disposal. Try a tickle."

"A tickle?" said Bruce. "OK..."

Jet aimed another punch at him, but Bruce grabbed his paw and quickly tickled him under the arm. Jet suddenly went limp. He giggled and looked at Bruce like someone who had just woken up from a deep sleep.

"What is this?" demanded the Ringmaster.

"Master Stalking also taught me how to release those under the spell of the Roar of Victory," said Chuck. "You see, laughter is a powerful weapon, Ringmaster. Something your clowns would know nothing about."

"Eh, we're funny," said Sheffield.

"Aye, that sea joke I told earlier was pretty good," said Grimsby.

"What happened? What's going on?" asked Jet, rubbing his head. "And why are you holding my paw, Bruce?"

Bruce released him. "You were under the Roar of Victory spell, but I tickled you and you're all right now. Right, it's time to get some goons."

"Fair enough. Let's go!" cried Jet.

"Before the Clan, each enemy cowers, for now we fight till victory is ours," said Chuck.

The ninja meerkats bowed gracefully, then set about kicking, punching, slicing, whacking, thwacking and just about every other word you can think of for fighting. Jet grabbed Doris by the tail and swung her around, sending her flying into the two clowns. Meanwhile, Chuck, Donnie and Bruce took on the evil trapeze artists. Chuck leaped into the air and cut through their swings with his sword, sending them tumbling to the ground where Donnie and Bruce were waiting.

Soon all seven Von Trapezes were in a tangled mess on the ground, along with the clowns and Doris the Dancing Dog.

"And now for the Ringmaster," said Chuck.

But in the chaos of the fight, the Ringmaster had already vanished.

"How does he always do that?" snarled Jet.

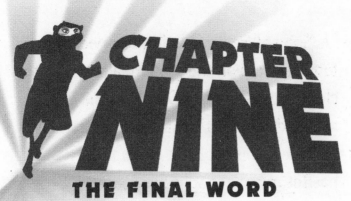

CHAPTER NINE

THE FINAL WORD

"Well, in spite of a slight technical hitch with the speaker system that caused it to cut out on the stroke of midnight, it's been a spectacular night of celebrations here in Hong Kong to bring in the Year of the Tiger," said a news reporter on a huge TV screen.

The meerkats were on the other side of Hong Kong harbour, walking along the Avenue of Stars, which was lined with the names of famous actors and actresses, including the greatest kung fu film stars.

"Look, Jackie Chan," said Bruce excitedly.

"Take a photo of me with this one."

Behind them the TV screen continued showing the news report. "And the good news is that Ming, the speckle-white tigress who went missing from Hong Kong Zoo, has returned, although the reason for her disappearance and the circumstances surrounding her return remain a mystery."

"Can't we take the credit just this once?" asked Jet.

"No," replied Chuck. "True ninjas do not seek glory or thanks. The satisfaction of a job well done should be enough for you. Besides, it's best we do not draw attention to Ming. No one else must discover her true power."

Donnie nodded in agreement. "She's no mere cat," he said.

"That's right. *We* are meerkats," said Bruce.

The others groaned.

"What?" asked Bruce. "I don't get it."

"Come on," said Chuck. "I'll explain it on the way home."

CHUCK
COBRACRUSHER

Leader of the Clan
(and the brains)

Specialist ninja skill:
Nifty with the sword
Most likely to be heard saying:
Before the Clan, each enemy cowers,
for now we fight till victory is ours!
Most likely to be found:
Meditating or practising his sword-play
(though not at the same time)
Famous for:
Remaining calm under pressure

SMALL. FURRY. DEADLY.

NINJA MEERKATS

JET
FLASHFEET

Super fast ninja
A lean, mean fighting machine

Specialist ninja skill:
A dab hand with the nunchucks
Most likely to be heard saying:
Ninja-boom!
Most likely to be found:
Practising his moves and reading his
collection of magazines and books.
His favourites are *What Karate!*,
101 More Martial Arts Moves
and *Kung Fu Weekly*
Famous for:
His impetuous ways, which
can lead to trouble...

NINJA
MEERKATS

BRUCE
WILLOWHAMMER

aka Bruce "the muscle" Willowhammer
The clue's in the name, this fella is a mighty powerhouse of strength

Specialist ninja skill:
The throw – anytime, any place, anywhere ... anyone...

Most likely to be heard saying:
Time for some Bruce Force!

Most likely to be found:
Doing 100 press-ups whilst planning a BIG breakfast

Famous for:
His bottomless appetite

NINJA MEERKATS

DONNIE
DRAGONJAB

Brilliant inventor
and master of gadgets

Specialist ninja skill:
Being able to turn anything into
a deadly weapon

Most likely to be heard saying:
Something sarcastic

Most likely to be found:
Taking things apart, putting things
back together and devising cunning
disguises

Famous for:
His love of technology

NINJA MEERKATS

A legendary Indian **EMERALD** with mystical powers has been **STOLEN** from under the noses of the monkeys who guard it. The meerkats team up with kung fu supremo the **DELHI LLAMA** to investigate. Some **MONKEY BUSINESS** is going on and there's no prizes for guessing who's behind it ... the meerkats smell a rat in a **TOP HAT**.

IT'S TIME FOR THE
NINJA MEERKATS
TO LEAP INTO ACTION!

OUT NOW!

SMALL. FURRY. DEADLY.

NINJA MEERKATS

ESCAPE FROM ICE MOUNTAIN

GARETH P. JONES

VISIT THE AUTHOR'S WEBSITE AT:

www.garethwrites.co.uk